Long Live
Princess
Smartypants

PUFFIN BOOKS
Published by the Penguin Group: London, New York, Australia, Canada, India, New Zealand and South Africa
Penguin Books Ltd, Registered Offices: 80 Strand, London WC2R 0RL, England

www.penguin.com

Published 2004
1 3 5 7 9 10 8 6 4 2
Copyright © Babette Cole, 2004
All rights reserved
The moral right of the author/illustrator has been asserted
Made and printed in China
ISBN 0–141–38033–0

Long Live
Princess
Smartypants

Babette Cole

PUFFIN

Smartypants, Princess of Totaloonia,
loved playing with
baby dragons.

It would be nice to have
a baby of my own,
she thought . . .

as long as I
don't have to marry
some dumb prince!

She asked her parents if it was possible to have a baby without being married.

"Certainly NOT!" said her mother, the queen, who was busy knitting for her forthcoming art exhibition.

"And," she added, "I'm putting you in charge of the banquet for the Grand Opening of my show.

Make sure there's plenty of Royal Brown Gravy. The guests will love it!"

Princess Smartypants hated cooking, so she phoned the royal grocer for a packet of ready-mix brown gravy.

But the line was a bit crackly . . .

"Yes, Your Totalooniness. One packet of ready-mix BROWN BABY on the way!" said the grocer.

Princess Smartypants was in a hurry. She didn't read the label; she just followed the instructions on the back.

1. Mix contents with half a litre of milk.

2. Stir violently over a red-hot heat.

3. Add plenty of pepper.

4. Leave to 'rise'
under a damp cloth.

The result was

INCREDIBLE!

Princess Smartypants
forgot about the gravy!

She was DELIGHTED
with her new baby . . .
although he did seem unusually
strong for his age.

The baby wrecked the exhibition. The royal
dignitaries all fled in terror – except for
her wicked uncle . . .

the evil Count Rottenghut!

He snatched the baby . . .

and made off for Castle Creep, home of the despicable Prince Swashbuckle.

The prince had never forgiven Smartypants for refusing to marry him and turning him into a toad!

With Rottenghut's help, he had been plotting to take over Totaloonia ever since.

They thought the baby would be just
the secret weapon they needed!
  "What a delightful child,"
drooled Prince Swashbuckle.
"You have done well,
my friend."

Princess Smartypants summoned her mighty dragons.
   "We must rescue my baby!" she commanded.
"He is dangerous in the wrong hands!"
   "I know what a responsibility babies are,"
said Amazonia Sizzleflame, "I've had three thousand!"

So, with Amazonia
in the lead, the squadron
of dragons zoomed off.

The dragons breathed their
fiery breath upon the castle
until it glowed red hot!
Its evil occupants ran out
and were captured
at once.

Smartypants and Amazonia
flew in through one window
and out of another,
grabbing the baby
on the way.

"There you are," said Smartypants to her parents,
"I have saved Totaloonia from deadly peril!"

"Oh good," said her mother. "I'm glad you're
so brave, because you can rule . . .

while we take my exhibition on a world tour. And don't let that dreadful child destroy the kingdom while we're away!"

CRASH

Princess Smartypants soon found out that it was much easier to rule the kingdom than the baby . . .

Now that he knew his own strength, he was rapidly becoming the palace pest!

"Perhaps some people are just
not cut out to have babies,"
she sighed.

Then Princess Smartypants had a brilliant idea!
She asked Amazonia Sizzleflame if she
could have one of her eggs.
"Of course," said Amazonia. "I've got
far too many. Don't forget. You must
sleep on it for a week."

Poor Princess Smartypants didn't sleep a wink for a week!

But it was worth it!

The baby was very respectful of
his new brothers, Pongo and Bongo,
and he never misbehaved again!

So when her parents rang to ask how the ruling was going,
Princess Smartypants could honestly say,
"I've got every little thing
under control!"